I0517088

CHRISTMAS STORIES FOR EVERYBODY

2014

1st. Edition English

1st. Printing English

Copyright © Jette Steen

Cover: Jette Steen

English translation by

Word to Word

Kolding, Denmark

Translated from the 2nd edition in
Danish 2012

ISBN 978-87-93112-10-0

info@forlagetpetit.dk

— Forlaget —
PETIT

CHRISTMAS STORIES FOR EVERYBODY

Best told by candle light

To be read aloud at cosy moments with family and friends at Christmas time - may, of course, also be read at other times during the year and by oneself.

There are stories about philanthropy, morality, disappointment, joy and much more - but they all have one thing in common: They give food for thought, like for instance:

That we should take care of each other.
That not all of us have the same access to material goods and, therefore, we do not all have the same opportunities.
That many people, especially old people, feel let down and alone during Christmas.
That we should not throw suspicion on other people if we do not have proof.
That we should do our utmost not to hurt or disappoint other people, not only at Christmas time but all through the year.

Like me, you may have had stories like these read aloud to you when you were a child and maybe you recognise the rewarding feeling of togetherness when the whole family is sitting there, quietly listening.
This tradition and feeling I would hereby like to pass on to the younger generations.

I am lucky to have inherited some of these books, some of which were written as far back as 1923. And I have taken the liberty of letting myself be inspired by them and using them as point of departure for some of my own stories.

 **THANK YOU!**

Every year at Christmas time, the author gives popular readings of "Christmas Stories for Everybody…." at charitable events.

Contents

Lost in Münsterland

Ulrik and Camilla have decided to spend a weekend in Germany in December as Ulrik's job has required all his attention for the past two months and they haven't spent much time together. They are looking forward to going, and Ulrik is busy packing their station car with all the things you need when you are a family with two small children.

They leave shortly after, Ulrik behind the wheel, Camilla sitting next to him and Alice aged five and Viktor aged two in their safety seats at the back. Viktor is asleep and Alice asks impatiently, "Are we there, yet?"

Ulrik looks at her, reassuringly.

"Yes, it won't be long now.

Are you looking forward to the holiday?"

Alice doesn't answer.

She yawns loudly, leans back and closes her eyes.

They finally reach the hotel, which
looks extremely cosy, and Ulrik goes
into the reception while Camilla
checks on the luggage in the back of
the car.
Ulrik comes back with the keys and
Alice opens her eyes.
"Hurrah, we're here."
The parents take the children out of
the car, gather as much of the luggage
as they can carry and go up to their
room.
Alice jumps around in the beds,
singing and thinking everything is new
and exciting.
When they have finished unpacking and
have changed their clothes, they go
down to the restaurant and sit down at
a table.
Ulrik looks through the menu and
consults Maria about what to order.
Then he looks around and says, "It'll
be interesting to see whether granddad

was right when he suggested that we should go here for our holiday".
The owner of the hotel comes up to their table.
"Welcome. What would you like to eat?"
Ulrik orders the food and asks the owner about the region, places to see, activities for children, etc.
Meanwhile, Alice has left the table to say hello to the owner's little terrier.
Shortly after, the owner passes by the child and smiles.
Ulrik looks around.
He cannot see Alice anywhere, so he gets up and calls out for her.
"Alice, where are you?"
The owner winks her eye at him and nods towards the place on the floor where Alice is sitting padding the dog, and Ulrik turns to Camilla.
"Have you ever seen anything like this?

It looks like we have to buy her a dog soon."

Camilla gets up and looks in Alice's direction, smiling.

"Yes, that's really amazing.

Where did she learn that?"

Ulrik looks firmly at her.

"Actually, it's not so strange.

She has been used to a small dog like this since she was a baby and my mum and dad were looking after her".

Camilla listens and answers thoughtfully, "Well, yes, but still."

The owner passes by Alice with a tray, smiles and whispers to her with a knowing look, "There's a soda pop for you."

Alice looks up, runs to the table and sits down.

Ulrik looks inquiringly at her.

"What have you been up to, Alice?"

Alice laughs.

"The lady said something to me, but I didn't quite understand what it was."
Camilla and Ulrik laugh, and the owner returns with their food, and they start to eat.
Alice is eating eagerly.
"Yummi. It tastes good."
Ulrik, who must have been very hungry, too, falls on the food.
"Yes, doesn't it.
They make really good food here."
They eat quietly and when nobody can get another bite down, they return to their room.

The next morning, Camilla is walking towards the car pushing little Viktor in his pushchair, and Ulrik comes shortly after.
Camilla turns to Ulrik, puzzled.
"Where is Alice?"
Ulrik looks around and walks into the hotel again where the owner smiles at

him and points to a place on the
floor.

Ulrik walks over there and finds Alice
together with the little dog.

He explains to Alice that they have to
go, but they will be back so that she
can say hello to the dog again, and a
little later Ulrik and Alice walk hand
in hand out of the hotel, and Ulrik is
smiling.

"Apparently, she had to say goodbye to
the dog first."

They all get into the car and drive
off, and Ulrik says, "I think that we
should visit the church granddad told
us about."

He drives into a parking lot, parks
the car, and the family gets out.
Camilla puts Viktor back in his
pushchair, and Ulrik takes Alice by
the hand.

On their way towards the church, they pass a large fountain, and they stop to look at it.

Alice is very interested in the fountain and can hardly be dragged away from it, but Ulrik tugs at her arm and they continue into the church.

Inside the church, Ulrik immediately picks up a brochure and takes a look around before they walk towards the altar.

There are no other visitors, but in the aisle a cleaning lady is washing the floor.

It is chilly in the church, and Camilla gives Viktor a sweater on while Ulrik is looking closely at the altarpiece, then in the brochure and then back at the altarpiece.

A streak of light falls on Alice from the side where a cleaning lady is passing with a bucket, and she sees a

small door in the side wall of the
church.
She walks over there and sees a poor
little dog outside gasping for breath,
and she goes through the door.
The dog practically drags itself over
to a tree where it lies down, and
Alice follows it.
"Poor little thing, are you thirsty?"
"Look, I brought you some water."
She takes off the small water bottle
which is hanging around her neck,
lifts up the dog's head and starts
feeding it water.
Shortly after, she shakes the empty
bottle.
She strokes the dog and starts walking
towards the fountain where she tries
to fill the bottle, which is not
particularly easy, as the jets which
come pouring down are rather thick,
but finally she succeeds.
Ulrik is studying the altarpiece.

"My dad was right when he called this altarpiece amazing."
He turns around and Camilla looks up.
Suddenly, Ulrik looks around the church with a worried expression on his face.
"Where is she?
Where is Alice?"
Camilla looks at him, annoyed, and pushes the pushchair with Viktor towards him.
"I thought you were holding her hand?"
Ulrik calls out gently.
"Alice, Alice where are you?"
He and Camilla look all over the church, and Camilla is close to tears when she says, "She is not here.
But where on earth can she be?"
Ulrik has a determined look on his face when he says, "But she must be here somewhere."

Ulrik goes to the side of the church,
and shortly after he looks quite
desperate and starts to shout.
"Alice. Alice come to dad."
A parish clerk comes up to them and
looks inquiringly at the visitors.
"Is something the matter?"
"Are you missing somebody?"
Ulrik looks at the clerk, confused and
guilt-ridden.
"Yes, our daughter.
She was standing here right next to
me."
Camilla looks behind the altar, and
the clerk looks at Ulrik and asks,
"How long ago was that?"
"But I was just looking at the
brochure for a short while, but now it
must be five or ten minutes ago, I
suppose."
"Just a moment."
The clerk goes through the door next
to the altar, and a little later he

comes out followed by three other
people.

He looks insistently at them and
points.

"Okay, you go upstairs, and you look
in the basement, while you go round
the back to look.

Are we clear?"

The three assistants nod and disappear
in different directions.

A little later, the three of them
return shaking their heads, and the
clerk gives them new orders.

One of them is searching the area
around the fountain.

He asks the passers-by whether they
have seen Alice, and finally he
approaches a married couple.

"Excuse me.

Have you seen a little fair-haired
girl with pigtails?"

The woman looks at him, astonished.

"No, has she gone missing?"

"Yes, one moment she was standing next to her dad in the church holding his hand, the next she was gone."
The man looks calmly at him.
"But then she must still be inside the church?"
"No, we have looked everywhere."
The woman puts her hand to her mouth.
"That's just awful.
And in this day and age when you hear so many terrible things happen.
Have you called the police?"
"No, but I suppose we'll have to now, will you ask around?"
"Yes, of course."
The couple approaches the other people outside the church and talks to them, and soon they are all searching the area.
The assistant returns to the church, shaking his head.
"I have asked some people in the square.

It seems that nobody has seen her, but they are looking for her in the streets."

The clerk has a worried look on his face when he thanks the assistant and beckons Ulrik to follow him, and the clerk and Ulrik go through the door behind the altar while Camilla is left petrified on a bench at the front of the church.

The clerk picks up the phone and dials while Ulrik is cringing next to him.

"Hallo. Yes, it's about a little girl who seems to have disappeared in this church.

No, she was standing next to her parents.

The father let go of her hand and the moment after she was gone.

Yes, we have searched through the entire church.

We have also talked to people outside
the church and they are now looking
for her.
Yes, thank you.
We would like that very much."
The clerk turns to Ulrik and tries to
look optimistic.
"The police are sending a dog patrol
right away."
Ulrik walks out the door and passes by
a cleaning lady who looks curiously at
him on her way out of the church.
He continues and without a word sits
down next to Camilla who is crying
now.
In the square by the fountain, a lot
of people have gathered and are
talking; one of them has jumped into
the fountain to look for Alice there.
Shortly after, some police officers
walk through the door with large
police dogs, and the clerk comes out
of his office to talk to them.

One of the officers turns to Ulrik and
Camilla.

"Do you have a piece of clothes or
something …?"

Camilla feverishly finds Alice's coat
at the bottom of the pushchair and
hands it to him.

The officers and their dogs gather
around Alice's coat before scattering
about the church but, apparently, one
of the dogs has already scented
something and is pulling its officer
towards a closed door at the side of
the church.

The officer calls out to the clerk.

"Do you have a key to this door?"

"Yes, but it's always locked."

"That may well be, but Kingo wants to
go out there, so you'd better find
it."

"Yes, I'll go and get it."

The clerk disappears into his office
and quickly returns with a large
bundle of keys.
He walks to the door and tries out
some of the keys.
Camilla, Ulrik and the sleeping Viktor
also approach the door which finally
opens.
Kingo immediately runs over to a tree.
They can hear another dog barking and
Ulrik hurries over there.
On a bench under the tree lies Alice,
fast asleep, with the little dog
proudly watching over her.
The dog licks her face and she wakes
up.
She cuddles the dog and looks
surprised at all the big dogs and the
police officers, and Ulrik picks her
up.
"You must never walk away from me
again.

We got so afraid when we couldn't find you."

She strokes the dog.

"But the dog was thirsty."

A police officer hands Alice's water bottle to Ulrik while winking his eye at him, and Camilla gives Alice a hug before the little family leaves the church.

As they pass by the fountain, Alice says,

"I fetched the water from here all by myself."

Ulrik and Camilla look doubtfully at the huge fountain, and Camilla says,

"Yes, I think that you have saved the little dog's life, but you must never again walk away without your daddy or me.

Promise?"

"Yes."

She laughs and jumps around the fountain while her parents watch her with a relieved smile on their faces.

The Thousand Kroner Note

15 year old Anja, who is one of four
siblings, is walking home from school
at her own quiet pace.

She stops at the red traffic light and
looks around.

Suddenly, someone shouts, "Hello Anja,
wait up."

Anja turns around and sees Kirsten
running towards her, and when she
reaches her, she says breathlessly,
"Well, there you are?

It's been an awful long time since we
have seen each other.

We never see you at the club anymore."

Anja tries deliberately to look very
grown up.

"No, I've had other things on my
mind."

Kirsten gives her a grin.

"Like what.

You haven't fallen in love, have you?"

"Oh, no."

Kirsten suddenly looks serious.

"How is your mum, by the way?
My mum says that she still hasn't come
back to work and that they have hired
a temp for an indefinite period of
time."
Anja looks away.
"No, she hasn't started work, yet.
She hasn't really been herself since
the assault."
"No, that was a terrible experience,
but can't she get any help?"
"Yes, she has tried that several
times.
She is still seeing a psychologist and
has joined several groups of people
who feel the same way she does.
But so far it hasn't helped her.
These things take time, I guess."
"I really feel sorry for her."
Anja looks inquiringly at Kirsten.
"And how are things with you?
Has Helene moved out yet?"

"Yes, she did that already last summer.
She now lives in Copenhagen and is studying communication or something."
Anja nods and smiles.
"Yes, she always knew what she wanted. But tell me, didn't she use to help out in the toyshop?"
Kirsten laughs uneasily.
"Yes, why?"
"Because I've been thinking that it would be nice to have a Christmas job like she did."
"Ha, you can forget about that.
You have to be 16 to get a job like that.
And why on earth would you want that for?
Do you know how many hours you have to work?"
The girls cross the road and walk on a little further until Anja has to turn down a side road to get home.

They say a quick goodbye and agree to see each other again soon.

Anja lets herself into the house, shouts, "It's me", and continues into the living room where her mum is sitting in her armchair doing nothing as usual.

Her face lights up when she sees Anja. "Hi my dear, did you have a nice day at school?"

"Yes, it was okay."

Anja gives her mum a quick hug and asks her if she can get her anything, then continues upstairs to her room where she turns on the stereo and lies down on her bed, staring into the air and thinking.

The day before, she had overheard a conversation between her mum and dad, and her dad had said that they could only stay in the house till after Christmas, and then where would they go?

She is lying there worrying, imagining that they will have to move to the large barracks where one of her classmates lives.

The flats are very small, and a lot of troublemakers live there.

And there's always a foul smell in the stairway.

She shakes her head, unable to believe that things would really go so wrong.

She goes downstairs again and looks at the purse and shopping list on the kitchen table, then puts on her coat and pops her head into the living room where her mum is sitting.

"I'm going shopping then, do you need anything else?"

Her mum looks up and shakes her head, but then she suddenly looks inquiringly at Anja.

"Oh yes, it's Thursday today, isn't it?"

Anja smiles indulgently.

"Yes mum, today is Thursday.
Do want me to buy the weekly for you?"
The lines on her mum's forehead
smoothen as she smiles at her
daughter.
"Yes, thank you.
I would like that very much."
Anja goes to the store to shop and
quickly returns.
She hands her mum the magazine and
goes into the kitchen to do the things
her dad has told her to do after her
mum was taken ill.
She empties the dustbin, washes the
dishes and peels potatoes and then
goes upstairs to her room again and
sits down at the desk to do her
homework.
There's a big noise downstairs.
It's her older brother, Nikolaj, who
returns home from work.
He is almost 19 and started as an
apprentice electrician a couple of

months ago to their parents' great
regret, as they would have liked him
to continue his studies after primary
school.
But that was not for Nikolaj who had
always been fiddling with the
electrical appliances in the house,
and that seemed to be his only
interest.
He occupied most of the basement, and
the day he started at the
electrician's shop their dad said that
he had to pay for living at home.
But that was okay, she thought,
because Nikolaj seemed to earn quite a
lot of money.
Shortly after, she hears her dad's car
stop in front of the house.
She tries to concentrate on her
homework but is disturbed again and
again by the sound of Nikolaj and
their dad discussing, even though she

cannot hear what they are talking
about.

A little later, she hears the front
door slamming and looks out the
window.

Nikolaj pulls the hood of his sweater
over his head as he walks away.

She can hear the twins on the stairs,
and shortly after the door opens and
the two little rascals aged eight come
into her room to say hello.

Then, her dad enters and asks her if
she has had a good day and if she has
time to help him prepare, and the four
of them go downstairs to cook.

They sit down to eat and watch
television, and nobody mentions
Nikolaj.

Anja clears the table and then
disappears upstairs to her room
without a sound to continue with her
homework.

The twins come to say goodnight, and shortly after Anja again hears loud voices from the living room.

This time, she decides to go out on the staircase to try to hear what's actually being said.

"Listen, Lene, it may well be that you are not feeling well and that you are anxious all the time.

I'm quite sure that a lot of other people feel the same way, but they pull themselves together.

You really need to pull yourself together, too. Forget about it all and come back to reality.

Your family needs you.

The twins as well as me.

Yes, and Nikolaj and Anja.

You know they do.

Otherwise, we'll have to put the house up for sale now."

"But Anton.

Do you really think I like sitting
here?
You know that the doctors say I'm
suffering from an anxiety neurosis and
that seeing the psychologist will help
me.
I believe that too, but like they say,
it's going to take a while."
Her dad snaps, "Time, all right.
No, all they want is our money.
But I can tell you as much as this.
In the future we won't be able to
afford that, either."
Anja can hear her dad coming into the
hallway and she hurries into her room.
She sits down at her desk and looks at
the essay in front of her, but it's
useless to think that she can
concentrate on that now, so she turns
on the music and lies down on her bed
with her diary.
A little later, she goes down to get a
glass of water, and from the living

room she can hear her mum crying and
sniffing quietly, but she doesn't go
in there, instead she tiptoes back to
her room.

The next day, Anja makes a decision on
her way home from school.
It's make or break, I have to try, she
thinks and turns into the street where
the toyshop is.
She asks to see Mr Holmegaard, the
manager.
As she expected, Mr Holmegaard
explains to her that she has to be 16
before he can hire her, but as they
are standing there talking, Marianne,
Kirsten's mum, passes by.
Mr Holmegaard smiles and greets her
and asks her about Helene.
Marianne tells him that Helene has
settled in well in Copenhagen, but
suddenly she turns to Anja and says
that she is very sorry that Anja's mum

is still not well, and would Anja
please give her Marianne's best
regards.
Then she disappears with some excuse
about being busy.
Mr Holmegaard looks at Anja with
surprise.
"What's wrong with your mum?
"Yes, please excuse me for asking but
I went to school with your mum and
Marianne."
Anja tells him about how her mum was
attacked one day after closing time in
the clothing shop where she works.
She was the last person left in the
shop and had just finished balancing
the cash and putting the money in the
bag to take it to the safe-deposit
box, when some men pried the door open
and broke into the shop.
Mr Holmegaard touches her shoulder and
says, "Oh, no", while he gently pushes

her towards his office where he points
to a chair and asks her to sit down.
Then he looks at her with sad eyes.
"What happened to her?"
Anja suddenly looks up at him,
embarrassed, and her voice is
trembling slightly.
"I think they tried to rape her while
they were filling clothes into some
big sacks, and then they ran off with
an entire week's turnover."
"And how long ago was that?"
"It must be about six months ago by
now."
"Mr Holmegaard asks her whether Lene
is getting any help and talks for a
long time about all the bandits who
think they are free to ruin other
peoples' lives and take what they
want, and then he looks seriously at
Anja.
A little later, Anja leaves the shop,
all excited.

She has made an agreement with Mr Holmegaard that she should start by helping out in the two afternoons a week when she gets off early from school, and later she will become part of the Christmas staff.

Anja hurries home.

Her mum sits languidly in the living room, and Anja continues upstairs to her room.

She sits down and starts to work out how much she will be able to earn.

Then she does her homework.

Later, when the family is having dinner in a tense atmosphere, she breaks the good news and tells about her job as Christmas helper.

Nikolaj laughs.

"I suppose that means larger Christmas presents this year?"

"Don't count on it, I intend to save up."

"And for what, if I may ask?"

"It's a good thing to have savings when you move away from home."
"Ha, well, that won't happen in the immediate future, little sister."
Her dad doesn't say a word, but her mum says that she thinks it sounds like a sensible thing to do.

Already the following week, when Anja is off early from school, she starts her job in the toyshop.
At first, she is just given all the boring tasks such as filling up the shelves with toys from the storeroom, but eventually she is also allowed to price-mark the toys.
About the time when the Christmas shopping starts, she has become so familiar with everything that she is also serving the customers and operating the till.

She is proud when she receives her
first pay, and she buys some flowers
for her mum.
Her mum is pleased, but her dad
explains to her that she should have
spent her money on more useful things.
Anja looks defiantly at her dad, then
at her mum.
"Isn't it a long time since you have
seen the psychologist, mum?"
Her mum looks away immediately, while
her dad shrugs his shoulders.
"We have decided that your mum should
no longer see him, it doesn't help,
anyway."
"Doesn't it?"
"Well, I can mention a few examples of
how it has helped someone."
Her dad answers her angrily,
"Well, that's for us to decide and
beside we can't afford it now when
your mum is not earning so much
money."

Anja stares him in the eyes and says that she will be happy to help them pay for a session at the psychologist's, and her dad leaves the room with a shake of his head.

The next day, Anja and her mum make a new appointment with the psychologist.

Mr Holmegaard has hired two young men of 17 to handle the hard work in the storeroom and therefore, as November moves on, Anja spends more time serving customers.

And when December comes, she doesn't help in the storeroom at all anymore. But she still joins them for her afternoon meal because they are the same age as her, and the rest of the staff is between 20 and 30 years older.

Some days are so busy that they stand on each other's toes at the till.

One of these very busy days, one of her colleagues, Jane, aged 34, asks Anja to pick up some pizza for her when she goes for her break.
Anja looks astonished at her, and Jane, who is in a bad mood, says, "Well, that shouldn't be too much to ask, it can't be that difficult.
I have seen that you eat together with Anders and Bo every day and that you usually buy takeaway from the shop on the corner."
Anja looks down.
"Yes, they do and I'll ask them to bring something for you."

The following week, on her way to work, Anja buys a scratch card, and for the first time in her life she wins no less than one thousand kroner.
So she decides that today she will treat herself to junk food like the others.

It is an incredibly busy day in the toyshop, and everybody is standing on each other's toes, but at mealtime Anja takes the one thousand kroner note from her bag and follows Anders and Bo to the nice man on the corner to buy pizza.

When Anja returns, Jane is in despair over the many customers in the shop, and she immediately tells Anja off for returning late from her break.

Anja explains that she has held as long a break as she is entitled to while Jane is looking annoyed at her.

At the end of the day when things have calmed down and the many customers have vanished like snow in the sun, Mr Holmegaard comes out from his office and offers all of them a soft drink because they have already reached this month's turnover, so they go to the backroom to talk and relax.

Eva, who is about 50 years old,
usually balances the cash, but she has
got off early because today is her
birthday, so Jane does it instead.
A little later, she joins the others
in the backroom and says that she
cannot understand it but one thousand
kroner are missing from the till.
Bo immediately says that one thousand
kroner is a strange amount, and Jane
looks suspiciously at him and asks,
"Why"?
Bo looks at the others and says,
"Well, it would be easier to
understand if it was a hundred kroner
note because someone had given the
wrong change on a five hundred kroner
note or a thousand kroner note - but a
thousand kroner note?"
Mr Holmegaard nods and asks whether
she is absolutely certain, and she
goes into the shop to get the tape
from the till.

Except for a few purchases for a
couple of hundred kroner each, most of
the purchases that day have been made
with credit cards, and Mr Holmegaard
shakes his head and says that it's
very strange, indeed.
A couple of days later, exactly the
same thing happens.
Once more, exactly one thousand kroner
is missing from till, and suddenly the
atmosphere gets rather tense.
But when it happens for the third time
and Mr Holmegaard says that, surely,
this cannot be a coincidence, they all
feel under suspicion.

The next day when Anja comes into the
shop, Jane is talking to Mr Holmegaard
in his office.
She startles when Anja enters to put
down her bag, and Anja gets a bad
feeling when Mr Holmegaard looks
inquiringly at her.

Later that day, she sees that Bo and Anders have also been called to Mr Holmegaard's office and then, shortly before closing time, it is her turn. She is very tense when she sits down on the edge of the chair opposite Mr Holmegaard's desk.

He looks at her with such a sad expression on this face that she almost falls off the chair.

"I'm terribly sorry, I know that you have a hard time at home these days, but …"

He coughs and obviously finds it difficult to continue, until he straightens his back in the chair behind the desk and says without looking at her,

"Well, I might as well tell you how it was discovered, unless you already know?"

Anja stares thunderstruck at Mr Holmegaard.

"Know what?"

"Well, Jane had seen you with a thousand kroner note in your hand, and she told me that you had said to her that you always brought your own food because you couldn't afford this kind of excesses.

And the day when a thousand kroner note was missing for the first time, you suddenly went with Bo and Anders to eat pizza.

You see, I have also talked with Bo and Anders about it and they confirmed that you paid with a thousand kroner note."

Anja looks at him with dismay.

"But I had won that money."

Mr Holmegaard looks at her with sad eyes and says quietly, "I'm sure you understand, Anja, that there's nothing else for me to do than ask you to get your things and go home.

I can't have you here anymore."

Anja gets up and quickly fetches her bag and coat before she hurries out of the shop with tears running down her face.

She immediately runs home and upstairs to her room where she throws herself on the bed and cries her heart out, while she keeps asking herself how they could all believe that she could do such a thing.

At the dinner table that evening, she just tells her family that with only a few days till Christmas, they no longer need her help in the shop.

But she finds it difficult to hide her disappointment.

She is incredibly annoyed.

It was precisely this last week before Christmas, during her Christmas break from school, that she should have worked a lot and earned the most money.

The next few days, Anja sleeps most of the day away and cannot be bothered to take part in anything, until the night before Christmas Eve when the rest of the family is visiting relatives and the doorbell rings.

Mr Holmegaard is standing outside looking very embarrassed.

He apologises, asks her to forgive him and says, "Yesterday, another thousand kroner note was missing; as I just didn't understand how this could happen again, I pulled heavily at the till drawer, and the corner of a banknote appeared, and when I got the whole drawer out, I found four thousand kroner notes.

It turns out, you see, that in the compartment where we put the thousand kroner notes, on top of the stiff gift vouchers, the pile of notes suddenly got too high, which made the uppermost note fall down behind the drawer."

He hugs her and she cries with relief.
Then he hands her a parcel and says
that this is an apology from all her
colleagues who never really believed
that she did it, anyway.
Then he gives her an envelope with her
pay slip and a thousand kroner note
which he takes out of his pocket, "And
this is from me, you really deserve
it.
And I was thinking whether you would
like to help out in the shop between
Christmas and New Year's Eve and maybe
one day a week in the new year.
You know, I was really happy to have
you in the shop, you were a quick
worker and a fast learner."
Anja thanks Mr Holmegaard who hugs her
and wishes her and her family a happy
Christmas before she closes the door.
She immediately opens the envelope and
sees on the pay slip that she has also

been paid for the days she had to stay
at home.

She goes upstairs to her room and
takes the empty Christmas cards on her
desk and starts to write.

"For Dad. This is a small contribution
to our Christmas".

She puts the card and some money in
the envelope.

On another card, she writes, "For Mum.
I hope that this amount will buy you
all the help you need."

She dances around the room, cheering.
After all, everything had turned out
just the way she imagined.

The Ski Trip

The schoolyard is humming with life on this day in August when Lise is starting in the new school.

Her family - mum, dad and younger brother - have just moved to town a month ago, and Lise has not yet found any friends as the children in the neighbourhood are somewhat younger than her.

She is excited when she enters the classroom where she has been told to go; some of her new classmates in the seventh grade have already arrived.

She is standing a little shy just inside the door while the other pupils are looking curiously at her.

Suddenly, the door slams open and Lars and Jesper tumble noisily into the classroom, then they quickly sit down at one of the tables at the back of the room.

Malene and her best friend, Jessica, come walking through the door arm in

arm, and Lars and Jesper whistle from
the back of the room while the two
girls sit down at one of the tables at
the front.
Finally, their teacher, Linda, turns
up.
"Good morning, everybody.
"Well, did you have a nice holiday?"
She looks around and sees Lise.
"And you must be Lise, welcome.
I think you can sit here."
Linda points to a table behind Malene
and Jessica and Lise sits down.
Linda starts out quickly by asking
whether they can remember that before
the summer holidays they agreed to
start the new school year by writing
an essay about how they had spent
their holidays.
She hands out some booklets.
Shortly after, they are all writing
and Lise is thinking hard.

What on earth should she write about?
She cannot write that she and her
family had to move to Nyborg because
they couldn't afford the house they
were living in in Odense, and that
nothing else has happened during the
entire summer.
Moving, painting, cleaning, etc.
Linda leaves the classroom, and
suddenly Anders says.
"How the hell do you spell Lido de
Jesolo?"
Some of the pupils laugh while Jessica
turns around and asks him whether he
also went there during his holiday,
and then she tells him how it is
spelt.
And suddenly they are all telling each
other about places they have been, and
Malene turns around and looks at Lise.
"And where did you go?"

Lise cringes and doesn't really know
what to answer when, fortunately,
Linda comes into the classroom again.
"EH, I think I said that you should
write an essay, not give a lecture on
what you have been doing during the
holidays.
But perhaps it's appropriate to stop
here, then you can finish the essay at
home.
You don't have to hand it in until
Thursday.
And I have quite a few pieces of
information for you.
First of all, I have promised the
headmaster to remind you that the
selection for the school's swimming
tournament is in two weeks, and those
of you who think you are good enough
to participate should write your name
on the list hanging by the office.
But another important thing is our ski
trip to Val d'Isere in week no. 6.

I have the list of payments here so that each of you can see how much you still need to pay or whether you need to pay anything at all."

Linda looks through the list before she continues, "Well, most of you have paid the total amount.

It's only those of you who have decided to pay a monthly instalment that still need to pay a little.

But remember that the balance must be paid by the fifteenth of December."

The bell rings and the pupils rush out into the schoolyard.

Lise would like to know how much they have to pay for this ski holiday, but then she thinks that she probably wouldn't be able to afford it, anyway.

Some of her classmates ask her if she plays any sports.

She tells them about the sports she played in Odense and is fairly quickly accepted.

The rest of the school day is nice and quiet even though she has to be introduced to the other teachers, as well.

A week later, as Lise and Malene are passing by the office, Malene stops and says to Lise, "You mustn't forget to sign up for the swimming tournament; it would be great if we could win this year."
Lise looks at the list, a little uneasy.
"But I don't know how good I am compared to the other contestants?"
"Well, no. But if you were on the winning team at the other school, you must be fairly good, even though you never know if you'll win, of course."
She hands the pen which is hanging next to the list to Lise who signs up.
As time passes, Lise feels that she has settled in well with the class

and, what is more, she has got herself
a job sorting bottles in the local
supermarket.
This way, she hopes to be able to earn
enough money to go on the ski trip.

On the day of the selection for the
school swimming tournament, Lise is
lucky and finishes in a fantastic
time, which she receives great credit
for.
And everybody tells her that they have
high expectations for her.
Shortly after, Malene tells her that
it is her birthday next month and that
she would like to invite Lise to a
small get-together for girls only.
Lise is very pleased with the
invitation and accepts it right away.

On the Saturday of Marlene's birthday
party, Lise is wandering aimlessly

about the house pondering what to
bring as a birthday present.
She needs to bring something.
She has no money because she has not
received her first pay yet, and she is
afraid to ask her parents.
Suddenly, she remembers the funny
gloves in fluorescent colours which
they found when they moved in.
They were still in their original
plastic bag, and she had been thinking
that she might use them herself, but
they were an ideal present for Malene.
She finds them, wraps them and sets
off to find the address which Malene
has given her.
She walks past a large, mansion-like
house but then realises that she has
walked too far.
She turns around and walks back,
wondering whether this could really be
the house Malene was living in.

Then her parents must be stinking rich.

At that very moment, Jessica comes round the corner, waves and walks familiarly through the large iron gate, up the paved path with flags, up lined to the front door and rings the bell.

The door is opened and Malene's mum greets them before leading them into an overwhelming hallway.

She gives the girls an appraising look while she goes to the staircase and calls Malene, telling her that her guests have arrived.

For a moment, Lise is thinking that, fortunately, none of the others have ever been to her house and seen her mum, who is always dressed in a jogging suit, and how they are living. Her thoughts are interrupted by Malene who comes running down the stairs to greet them.

She gabbles on and immediately shows
them into the dining room with the
splendidly laid dinner table.
She shows them the gift table and
says, "Look what I've got."
On the table are a pair of brand new
ski boots next to a posh ski suit,
some exquisite tops, a handbag and a
great deal of books and other things.
Jessica hands Malene a nicely wrapped
parcel while she looks at the gifts
and says that Malene has really been
spoiled for her birthday.
Malene opens the parcel and almost
screams.
"No, you didn't?
- You bought it anyway."
Malene hugs Jessica while she cries
out in a high-pitched voice, "It's one
of those posh Gucci purses.
We looked at them when we were window
shopping the other day, and I said
that I wanted one for my birthday.

- But I never imagined that you would buy it, Jessica.
Thank's a lot."
She hugs her friend again while Lise is asking herself whether she should pretend that she has forgotten the present and then try to borrow some money to buy something else.
Then Malene turns to Lise in anticipation.
Lise hands her the present and says congratulations, and Malene unwraps it, then smiles at her.
"Thank's, Lise."
Malene's dad comes through the front door dressed in a fantastic golfing outfit and immediately comes in to greet the girls, before he continues upstairs.
Malene's mum serves them drinks and places some snacks on a small table.
They sit down and Jessica has a lot to tell them because her cousin from the

States is visiting and, apparently,
she is a little in love with him.
While they are talking, Malene's dad
comes in, now wearing something quite
different.
It's a pair of jeans but they are far
more elegant than any pair of trousers
Lise has ever seen.
"Well, what are you drinking?"
He is sniffing at the jug on the table
when Malene's mum enters, smiling.
"No, I don't think there's enough
alcohol in it for you."
Malene's dad laughs and hugs Malene's
mum while Lise is watching with
surprise, thinking that her parents
never do that.
He walks up to the bar and pours a
drink for himself and Malene's mum,
then walks over to take a look at the
gift table.
He picks up the dainty purse from
Jessica and looks closely at it.

"Well, that's very nice, indeed.
It's very classy."
He opens it and looks at the tag
inside.
"Yes, I thought so.
Quality will tell.
It's a Gucci, of course."
He turns to Lise.
"And you must be the new girl that
Malene has been telling us about.
Where do you come from?"
Lise tells him that she and her family
come from Odense and then tries to
avoid his many questions by giving
very short answers.
Lise can hear a door opening and in
comes Malene's older brother, Joakim,
who is 18 years old and has just got
his driver's licence, and her six year
old younger sister, Belinda.
They politely shake hands with Lise
while tossing a casual hi to Jessica.

The phone rings and Malene's dad
answers it.

"Well, that's too bad.

- Yes, I will.

Yes, I'll give her your love, and get
well soon."

Malene looks inquiringly at her dad.

"Is Helene not coming?"

"No, unfortunately not.

She's still not better even though she
thought the whole day that she would
make it.

She sends her apologies.

But I think it's more important that
she gets well for your tournament next
week."

Malene's mum gets up.

"Well, then we might as well eat."

She leaves the room and Joakim follows
her.

Shortly after, Joakim comes in with a
tray with bowls and puts the bowls on
the table.

He goes out with the tray and returns
with soda pops in a small plaited
basket, and finally Malene's mum comes
in with a huge plate.
Malene's dad pours the wine and the
girls pour their soda pops, then they
say cheers and start to eat.
Later that evening, the girls are
sitting in Malene's room upstairs
listening to music and talking about
the approaching ski holiday.
Lise, who hasn't yet got her act
together to ask somebody about the
price of the trip, now asks the two
other girls, and Jessica immediately,
says, "Oh, it's not too expensive, I
think it's about 3,000 kroner.
You should hurry up and pay so you can
join us."
Lise quickly says that there's still
plenty of time until the fifteenth of
December while she asks herself how
she will be able to afford it.

She may just manage to earn enough money for the trip, but she also needs pocket money and she doesn't have any ski outfit, either.

At some point when Lise is out in the corridor looking for the toilet, she hears Belinda, who is apparently on her way to bed next door, saying that those ugly gloves looked like the ones she got last year and that they were outdated.

Lise feels that she can't really take part in the conversation anymore, partly because they are talking about things and places she doesn't know anything about, partly because she doesn't have any experience with boys. She says that she has to get up early the next morning, so she'd better go home.

They go downstairs, and she says goodbye to the girls and Malene's parents and is about to leave when

Joakim appears on the staircase and offers to drive her home.

He asks her where she lives, but she immediately says that it's not far and that, in fact, it's much easier to walk.

In the time following the birthday party, Lise clearly feels that Malene and Jessica have something in common which she has no part in, but when she wins the crawl and secures the school's winning position in the swimming tournament, they are all overexcited and Malene and Jessica ask her come to the cinema with them in the afternoon.

Lise explains that she can't really come because she has to look after her younger brother, but they keep pressing her and say that he can come, too.

Finally, she tells them that she's been lying and that the fact is that she has a job after school.

On the first of December when she gets her pay from the supermarket, she sits down and counts her money once more. She has two thousand and two hundred kroner, and of this amount she needs about two hundred kroner for Christmas presents.

But if she can earn another fifteen hundred kroner before week no. 6, then she can just about afford the ski trip and has five hundred kroner spending money.

She sits a while thinking, remembering Jessica's words about less than fifteen hundred kroner not being enough.

The next day, she stops Linda in the doorway and asks her how much it really costs to participate in the ski trip.

Linda gives her a startled look.

"Oh no, hasn't anybody informed you about that.

I'm really sorry, but I totally forgot that you were new because you settled in so quickly and easily.

But the trip costs three thousand kroner."

She looks inquiringly at Lise who feels somewhat uneasy.

"Do you want to sign up?"

"Oh, I really don't know.

How much extra money do you think we need?"

Linda suddenly looks as if she has just thought of something and says in a happy voice that, by the way, the price includes ski rental, so if she brings her own skis, the total costs will be reduced accordingly.

"But I was thinking about pocket money and so on."

"Well, the price includes lift card and ski rental, apart from that you only need money for amusement.
- pocket money, you know."
Lise looks down.
"And are ski boots and ski clothes also included?"
Linda chuckles while she answers,
"No, ski clothes are not included, but the boots are included in the ski rental."
"Okay, I'll just think about it, then."
Lise hurries to the classroom.
In her lunch break, Linda joins one of her colleagues in the staff room and tells her that she cannot understand how she could forget to inform Lise, the new girl in the class, about the ski trip.
She feels really bad because she got the feeling that Lise couldn't really afford it.

They talk about it for a while, and
the colleague who seems to be better
informed than Linda tells her that
Lise's parents moved to Nyborg because
her dad got a job there and that,
before that, he had been unemployed
for a long time.
But the day after he started his new
job, he was fired again, so money was
probably tight at home.
"By the way, what about the grant we
got?"
Linda looks at her in surprise while
she pulls out a binder from the rack.
"Oh yes, how was it with that money?"
They sit down close together and read.
"Yes, says the colleague, I thought
so.
You have received a joint grant, not
one per pupil.
How many are you?"
Linda takes out a list and counts.

"But after Ib and David left the school halfway through the previous school year, only eighteen pupils are going, and since the total price is forty five thousand kroner all inclusive, there's a balance of nine thousand."

"Yes, and that's exactly five hundred kroner per pupil."

"We could choose to spend it on the pupils while we are away, but, on the other hand, if we reduced the price, it might be possible for someone like Lise to join."

The following day, Linda tells the class that it has turned out that, in fact, the price for the trip is only two thousand five hundred kroner and that those who have already paid can choose to either leave the additional amount on the account and have it paid out as extra pocket money when they

leave for France or to have it paid
out now.

The same afternoon, Lise comes walking
down the street preoccupied with the
thought that she might be able to go
to France with the others, after all,
and thinking about how she'll be able
to afford some ski clothes because she
only has a coat that is too long and
no padded trousers.
She stops in front of a sports shop
which has ski suits hanging outside.
She touches the suits and looks at the
price.
Oh no, she thinks to herself, they are
much too expensive.
She turns around and is about to cross
the street when she suddenly sees a
car approaching at high speed straight
towards a little girl who is on her
way over the curb.

She takes a quick decision, grabs hold
of the girl and pulls her back onto
the pavement.
They both fall over, and the little
girl cries violently.
A man comes running out of the sports
shop and shouts, "What on earth?"
He picks up the little girl, who is
still crying, while people on the
pavement are telling each other how
Lise saved the girl with no thought
for herself.
Only after Lise has been helped on her
feet does she realise that the man is
Malene's dad and that the little girl
is Belinda.
He lays a hand on her shoulder and
asks her to follow him back into the
shop where he thanks her very much for
what she's done.
Then he asks her what in the world she
is doing here, at the complete
opposite side of town, and she

explains somewhat confused that she
had been to the bank, and as she
passed the sports shop, she was
wondering how much a ski suit costs as
this was crucial for whether she could
afford to join the others on the
pending ski trip.

A little later, Lise is on her way
home carrying a large bag with a ski
suit, ski gloves, a ski hat and a lot
of other stuff, and the next day she
can pay the two thousand five hundred
kroner for the ski trip knowing that
she has enough pocket money to take on
the trip.

Before the Christmas Holidays

Monday, the twenty second of December,
just two days before Christmas Eve,
when Jenny was downtown buying the
last Christmas present, she slipped in
to see an exhibition, which was held
in a large concrete building.
Jenny knew that she was late, the
exhibition closed at five p.m.
But she also knew that it would be
gone after Christmas and wouldn't come
again for a decade or so.
And she so wanted to see it.
At eighteen minutes to five, she
entered the exhibition room where she
seemed to be the only visitor.
While she was in there, she suddenly
had to go to the bathroom.
The ladies room was located at the end
of a long corridor, but Jenny was sure
she would make it.
She went quickly past a door behind
which she could hear loud music, and
she concluded that there must still be

82

people in the building; then she
continued down the corridor.
She threw her coat and bag on the sink
and went into one of the toilets.
But when she was ready to go out and
tried to unlock the door, she suddenly
had the lock in her hand.
She tried to pry the lock back in
place so that she could open the door
but didn't succeed.
She knocked on the door a couple of
times while pulling at the handle and
telling herself to calm down, somebody
would probably turn up soon.
Jenny looked at the iron door which
went all the way from the floor to the
ceiling, and she started to panic.
It was almost closing time, did
anybody know she was here?
The only sign of her was her coat and
bag in the room outside, and in her
bag was her mobile phone.

And it wasn't very likely that
somebody would use the toilets at this
time.
She suddenly felt the panic and
started hammering wildly on the door.
She was about to cry at the thought of
what could happen to her.
The place would be closed until next
Monday or maybe longer, and how would
she survive in there for eight days?
Jenny looked at her watch.
She had been stuck there for a quarter
of an hour now, and she continued to
hammer and knock like a madwoman.
Finally, she heard a timid woman's
voice asking her in broken Danish, "Is
anybody wrong?"
Jenny shouted in a shrill voice that
she was standing with the lock for the
toilet door in her hand and couldn't
get out, and the woman said that she
was the cleaning lady and that
everybody else had left.

Jenny asked her to phone somebody, but the woman didn't answer.

Jenny shouted, "Help me, please help me, I can't get out."

Nobody answered.

After a little while, the woman came back and shouted, "I try."

Jenny could hear her outside, prying with something, and asked her what she was doing.

Her head was pounding, and even though she was sure that now she would get help, she was still overwhelmed with fear.

The woman said, "I go get another", and Jenny was wondering whatever she meant by that.

She had just told her that nobody else was there.

Jenny shouted and asked the woman what she meant but didn't get any answer this time, either.

She could hear somebody tampering with the lock again, and suddenly the door flung open.

Jenny ran out, deeply shaken, and grabbed her bag.

She thanked the woman a thousand times for her efforts while looking admiringly at the fragile female figure with the tool box.

Shaking all over, Jenny went into the corridor and let the tears flow.

The woman followed her quietly to the entrance door which she unlocked to let her out.

Finally out in the street again, Jenny thought about how quickly things can go wrong and how careful you have to be.

And from now on, she never goes anywhere without having her mobile phone on her.

Unexpected Visitors

Sue and Torben live on a housing estate close to the Lakes in the City Centre of Copenhagen.

They have two small children, three year old Teodor and Michaela of eight months.

They are looking forward to visiting their parents and in-laws in Jutland over Christmas, and they are talking about how nice it's going to be.

Their parents and in-laws don't live very far from each other, so there's every reason to believe that it will be a lovely family Christmas.

They had hoped to be able to leave for Jutland on the twenty third of December but because of some problems at Torben's work, they don't take off until the twenty fourth.

Torben is outside packing and warming up the car when Sue's dad calls to ask when they are coming.

Sue explains that Torben has been at
work until two in the night, and
therefore they have decided not to
leave until now, at about half past
one.

Sue looks out the window and asks her
dad what the weather is like at their
end, and, apparently, it's not nearly
as bad in Jutland as it seems to be in
Copenhagen, so they agree that they
will probably arrive about three in
the afternoon, just in time for
afternoon coffee.

Torben carries out the rest of their
luggage, and Sue picks up Micaela and
takes Teodor by the hand and walks to
the car which is nice and warm,
fortunately.

Shortly after they have left, both
children are fast asleep in the
backseat.

Even though it's snowing a lot, the
motorway is still fairly clean and

passable, and they are driving at good
speed until Torben turns off to fill
up the car with petrol at a service
station close to Nyborg.

Sue asks him whether he would like a
cup of coffee and since the children
are asleep, they both go into the
shop.

They buy coffee to go, Danish and a
soft drink.

When they are about to pay, they
suddenly see on the TV screen hanging
behind the counter that somewhere in
Denmark there is so much drifting snow
that cars are overturned.

Sue is looking closely at the screen
while Torben is paying, and then she
asks one of the other customers,

"Is it on Bornholm again?"

"No, it seems to be in Jutland this
time."

Torben and Sue stays a little while to
be absolutely certain exactly where it

is, and before long they realise that
the pictures are from Aarhus.
They console themselves in the fact
that they are not going as far as
Aarhus and that even though the roads
looked quite unpassable when they
left, the motorways were far better.
Then they go back to the car.
Torben looks at his watch, it's only a
couple of minutes to three, and they
drink a little coffee before they
continue.
However, the farther they get, the
more it snows, and soon they can see
that there is also a lot of snow
drifting around on the Little Belt
Bridge.
And it gets worse with every
kilometre.
When they reach the bridge, Sue is
pointing terrified at a car lying in
the ditch.

A moment later, she sees another, and Torben is cursing and swearing about not being able to see anything.

He follows the taillights of the car in front of them hoping that the driver has better visibility than he, but just before the next town, the car skids.

He tries his best to manoeuvre the car, but soon they are stuck.

Sue looks worriedly at the children in the back, Teodor is about to wake up. She gives him his dummy and tucks him in.

Torben is outside shovelling snow away from the car wheels; then he tries to get the car moving again by driving forwards and backwards, but the car just seems to be sinking deeper and deeper into the snow.

Eventually, he takes the car mats and places them in front of the wheels.

Finally, the car starts moving, and Sue looks out of the rear window and asks, "What about the mats?"

Torben who has difficulties finding his bearings shouts, "To hell with them, the most important thing is that we got away from there."

Shortly after, he realises that they are going the wrong way and that they are on their way up the slip road.

He has no idea where he is and sees no immediate possibility of getting back on the motorway, so he continues for a while until the car starts snorting and then stops.

They look around, talking about what to do.

It starts getting cooler in the car, and when Micaela wakes up screaming and wakes Teodor, their little car suddenly turns into a hornet's nest. Teodor sits with his arms around his stomach, shaking.

"Mum, I'm really cold."

Sue tells him to snuggle down under the blanket.

Torben gets out of the car.

Sue calls her dad but there is no connection, and now she is really getting nervous.

If they cannot move, they'll freeze to death.

What a predicament they are in.

Torben comes back and says that they must all put on their boots and warm coats because they have to take a little walk, but Sue, who is now close to tears, refuses.

"You can't be serious, Torben?"

Isn't it what they always say, that you should stay in your car so you can be found?"

Torben sends her a nervous smile.

"Yes, but it'll quickly get too cold, and I have spoken to an elderly lady in that house over there where there's a light.

We are welcome to stay there and get warm while we are waiting for help."

Torben starts to help Teodor get his clothes on while Lene is looking around for the house.

"Where is it?"

Torben points in the direction of the house, and she suddenly sees a glimmer of light in the darkness.

She quickly puts on her boots and coat while she tells him that there is no telephone connection, and Torben answers that he already knows that.

Sue gets out of the car and tucks Micaela in the carry cot, and Torben carries Teodor on his shoulders, and then the four of them walk towards the light where a nice elderly woman welcomes them.

The little family go inside and take off their boots and coats before entering the woman's warm living room where they place themselves in front of the hot wood-burning stove.

She tells them to please make themselves comfortable and disappears into the kitchen.

Shortly after, she returns with some lemonade and then disappears again. This time, she returns with some cups, then with a jar of Christmas punch and, finally, she puts a dish with Danish doughnuts and some homemade raspberry marmalade on the table.

They look admiringly at all the things she has been able to conjure up in such a short time, and she asks them to please help themselves and to let her know if there's anything missing.

Sue asks if there is somewhere she can warm up a bottle of milk for Micaela

and if she can use the bathroom to
change Micaela's diaper.
Then she sits down and feeds the
bottle to Micaela.

Torben has been trying to use the
mobile again, but there is still no
connection, so he asks the elderly
woman, who now introduces herself as
Dagmar, if she has a land line he can
use.
She points to the telephone in the
corner and says, "Yes, by all means".
But her telephone is not working
either, and Torben sits down to drink
some punch and eat some doughnuts and
says, "What the heck do we do now?"
Dagmar says that at any rate they
mustn't try to drive on now and
explains that she has a spare room
where they can stay the night if it
should prove necessary.

"But, unfortunately, I haven't a lot of food in the house as I didn't expect any visitors", she says.

Sue and Torben look at each other and while Dagmar is in the kitchen to get more doughnuts, they agree that this is the best solution to the problem and that this Dagmar seems to be a very nice person.

Torben puts on his boots and coat and goes out the front door, and Teodor asks Sue if they are going to sleep here.

Sue nods, and he looks around the living room and asks Dagmar, whose only Christmas decoration is a single fir twig with some Christmas elves, whether she hasn't had the time to finish decorating the house for Christmas, yet.

Dagmar says that she is very sorry that she hasn't had the time then

winks her eye at Teodor and asks him
if he would please help her do it.
All excited, Teodor follows her into
one of the other rooms, and a little
later they come out with a large sack
whose contents they tip out on the
floor.
Dagmar and Teodor immediately start to
decorate for Christmas.
Torben returns with a lot of bags and
explains to Dagmar that she doesn't
have to worry about food, he will take
care of that as he had promised his
in-laws to bring a pre-roasted pork
loin for the Christmas dinner.
Dagmar goes into the spare room to
turn the heat on and says to Sue that
there is some clean linen in the chest
which she can put on the beds when the
room gets a little warmer.
Dagmar shows Torben into the kitchen
and tells him that she has potatoes,
red cabbage and a lot of other

ingredients which he is more than
welcome to put to use, if necessary.
Then she starts to lay the table while
Teodor decorates the rest of the
house, and Torben puts the pork loin
in the oven and makes Christmas
dinner.

Teodor comes into the kitchen and
asks, "What about the presents, dad?
Where are they?"

They go into the living room to find
the presents and, suddenly, Torben
sees the present for his uncle and
starts to unwrap it.

"Woops, see how lucky we are.
There's no better Christmas wine than
this one."

Sue claps her hands and Dagmar
approaches to take a look at the
bottle, as well.

A little later, they all sit around
the dinner table in the living room,
which is now filled with Christmas

elves, with a luxurious meal and
presents by the wood-burning stove.
They touch glasses and have a really
good time and when they finish eating,
Dagmar serves coffee and chocolates.
Teodor announces that he has always
thought that everybody had a Christmas
tree but with all these Christmas
elves, it really doesn't matter.
They sing Christmas carols and,
finally, Teodor gets his presents
which they all admire as he opens
them.

He asks Dagmar which present is from
her, and she says that she's sorry
but, unfortunately, she hasn't bought
one as she didn't know that he would
visit her for Christmas.

Torben immediately says that Dagmar's
present is the greatest because she
has invited them into her home so that
they could have a lovely Christmas Eve

together, and then he hands her a
present.

Dagmar opens it and says, "No, you
shouldn't have."

Torben laughs.

"Yes, we certainly should."
Our family gets lots of other
Christmas presents today, they'll just
get the ones from us a little later."

Dagmar takes the fancy tablecloth with
matching napkins out of the box and
thanks them soppily for the fine
present.

A little later, Sue goes into the
spare room to put linen on the beds
and shouts that it is nice and warm in
there now and that Teodor should come
and get his pyjamas on.

Teodor protests and says that he
certainly doesn't want to go to bed at
such an early hour, but he also says
that they must not forget to read him
his bedtime story.

Dagmar, who has entered the room, suggests that she should tell him a bedtime story about Christmas in the old days, so he quickly brushes his teeth and climbs into bed.

In the living room, Sue and Torben share Christmas presents and listen to Dagmar's sweet Christmas stories from the old days.

They are smiling and enjoying this lovely night.

Dagmar comes tiptoeing out of the room and says that Teodor has fallen asleep. Torben finds another present in the sack and opens it.

"How would you like a drop of Christmas brandy?"

Sue and Dagmar laugh and say, "Yes, please", and then they sit and talk for a long time by candlelight in front of the stove.

Dagmar tells them that she is 87 years old and has a daughter who lives in Australia.

She also has a grandchild, but she hasn't seen either of them since her seventy-fifth birthday.

She only talks with her daughter on the telephone on rare occasions.

She is married to some big hotel tycoon over there and even though they have a lot of money, they can't be bothered to visit her.

They finish their drinks and go to bed.

The next morning, the snow storm has calmed down but there is still a lot of snow on the roads.

Torben checks on the car while Sue and the children have breakfast with Dagmar.

It appears that the car has more or less landed in a huge snow drive so he

brushes away some of the snow before
opening the hood to take a closer look
at the various parts.

Then he shovels around the car and
gets inside it.

He is not very confident that he will
succeed in starting the car but feels
that he has to try, and to his great
surprise the engine starts to spin
immediately.

He carefully sets the car moving, and
shortly after he is on his way to
Dagmar's house where he leaves the car
with the engine on to keep it warm
while he goes inside to get the family
organised.

Torben and Sue pack their stuff in a
hurry and after bidding Dagmar a fond
farewell, the little family are again
on their way on Christmas holiday.

At ten a.m., they park outside Sue's
childhood home and her parents, who
have been deeply worried, greet them

happily and with great relief, asking
them how they have been.

During the afternoon, their mobiles
are working again so that they can
call and reassure Torben's parents,
too.

After telling his grandparents about
Dagmar's many Christmas elves and
Christmas in the old days, Teodor says
that next year Dagmar is going to
celebrate Christmas at their house.
Sue and Torben, who are in fact going
to arrange Christmas for the entire
family next year, look at each other
and Sue says, "But, of course."

And so she did.

Dad is Away on Business

Karin and Gunnar are sitting at the breakfast table when Anni comes down the stairs to have breakfast with her mum and dad.

Gunnar looks curiously at Anni.

"Are you on your way to a party?"

"No, sweet daddy, I'm not."

"But you look like someone who is going to a party."

Karin snaps good-humouredly at Gunnar, "Well, Gunnar, that's how young people look these days."

Gunnar grunts while he continues eating; at the same moment, Jesper comes whistling down the stairs.

He is in a hurry and grabs a roll on his way to the front door.

Karin turns to look at him.

"Young man, you have to get earlier out of bed in the morning, so that you have time to eat a proper breakfast."

"I know, but there was something I had to do first. See you."

The door slams and Jesper is gone.
Anni gets up, hurries off to get her
coat in the hallway and quickly
follows her brother while she shouts,
"Bye-bye."
Karin looks inquiringly at Gunnar.
"How long do you reckon it will take
this time, Gunnar?"
Gunnar looks at her over the edge of
his newspaper, and she continues, "You
know that we have been invited to
several events in the next couple of
weeks, and it would be nice if you
could participate together with the
rest of us.
The previous two years, the children
and I have been to the school's
Christmas party on our own.
By now, they probably all think that
we have been divorced or are living
separate lives."
Gunnar chuckles and lowers the
newspaper.

"Yes, but I expect to be back again on Friday, and then there'll be no more business trips this year."

Karin quickly clears the table, then gets her coat and kisses Gunnar goodbye.

"Well, have a nice trip, then. I'd better be off or I'll be late."

Gunnar looks at his watch and gets up.

"Yes, I'd better be off, too. Bye-bye."

Karin disappears out of the door and hurries to the fashion shop where she has been working for the past ten years, and Gunnar hurries off to the airport.

At about two in the afternoon, Karin enters the local butcher's shop.

She immediately recognises her neighbour in the line in front of her and approaches her to say hello.

"Hello, Gerda, how is Finn these days?"

Gerda smiles as she recognises Karin and says that her husband is still not well but that he is slowly recovering. The butcher asks Gerda what it'll be and she starts ordering, carefully pointing out each cut of meat.

Then she turns to Karin and asks her whether she and Gunnar would like to come over for a glass of wine and a little cheese on Friday night.

"It's been such a long time since we have talked, and Finn could do with a little company", she adds.

Karin accepts but mentions that she doesn't know for sure when Gunnar will be back from his business trip.

Gerda smiles and says, "Well, he's away again, is he?

Then let's say about eight o'clock, then he must be back, surely?"

Karin smiles and says, "Yes, I guess", and the butcher hands Gerda a bag and she pays.

Then the butcher turns to Karin, and Gerda slips out of the door.

A little later when Karin is doing the laundry, Anni comes home, all out of breath.
Karin looks up.
"Well, was it a tough bicycle ride?"
"It certainly was.
As from tomorrow, I'll definitely take the bus."
About six, Anni and Jesper are sitting at the table in the kitchen-dining area doing their homework, and Jesper asks if someone could please help him with his math.
Both Karin and Anni look at the assignment and shake their heads, and Karin returns to the kitchen to get dinner ready while she says, "I'm sorry, my boy.
They didn't teach us that kind of math at all when I was at school."

Jesper looks at his watch.

"Well, I'm sure dad knows."

Anni looks puzzled and asks him when he has to hand in the assignment and when he says that he doesn't have to hand it in until Thursday, she starts to laugh.

"But that's no use.

Dad's away on business."

Jesper looks at Karin who is lost in her own thoughts.

"How long will he be gone this time?"

Karin looks up.

"What? Who? Oh, dad.

He'll be back on Friday."

Anni, who is three years older than Jesper and is starting upper-secondary school next year, takes pity on her younger brother and helps him with his homework until dinner is ready.

The next couple days are business as usual, and Friday comes.

Karin has spoken to Gunnar on the phone, and he expects to be home about five in the afternoon, so she'll have dinner ready for half past six, at the latest.

At about three, Gunnar calls to tell her that the flight is delayed and that he has to catch the next one, which means that he won't be home until half past six.

However, the visit to Gerda and Finn's should still be okay.

However, as there seems to have been some incident at the airport because of which it has been decided to collect the passengers from various destinations on the same flight, the time of departure is postponed again.

Karin and the children have dinner, and she gets ready to visit Gerda and Finn.

There's no connection to Gunnar's
mobile, and she sits down, thinking
that he should be home any minute now.
But time goes by and when it's almost
half past eight, Karin calls Gerda and
says that she's sorry but Gunnar
hasn't come home yet and she doesn't
really know when he'll turn up.
Gerda, who has been arranging a cheese
table and made everything ready for
the guests, reassures her that it
doesn't matter if they come later, and
they agree that they should wait and
see for a little while longer.
When it's twenty past nine and Gunnar
still hasn't turned up, Karin calls
Gerda again and asks her whether they
can postpone the visit till another
day now that it's so late, and Gerda
agrees while she clearly expresses her
annoyance that all this lovely cheese
should go to waste just because Gunnar
is away on business yet again.

Gunnar calls Gerda from a cab and is
not home until half past ten.
All tired and grumpy.

On Saturday, they have arranged to
visit Karin's older sister who will be
celebrating Christmas with her
children and grandchildren and
therefore cannot join them on
Christmas Eve.
Both children have been looking
forward to the trip to Copenhagen, but
Gunnar is tired and not feeling well.
He sneezes and coughs and complains of
headache and fever, so Karin
reluctantly calls her sister and
cancels the trip.
On Sunday, she takes the children to
the shopping mall where they buy their
Christmas presents the last Sunday
before Christmas every year.
They usually continue to a place near
the wood to buy a Christmas tree, and

afterwards they eat at a little inn nearby.

But this time they drive directly back to the house, postpone the purchase of the Christmas tree and eat at home.

Gunnar is not well and can't be bothered to eat, which is not exactly how they had planned it, but there is nothing else to do than wait until he is feeling better.

Gunnar continues to be ill the next couple of days, and on Tuesday it's the school's Christmas celebration.

This year too, Karin has to take the children to the celebration alone, and the first person she greets looks inquiringly at her and asks if Gunnar is away on business again.

Karin notices the many prying eyes and is annoyed that this should happen again.

But for Pete's sake, the man can't help catching a cold, she thinks to herself, and that is what she tells all the curious parents.

Wednesday morning, Gunnar is feeling better and is sitting in the living room when the phone rings.

Shortly after, he calls Karin in the shop and tells her guilt-ridden that he has to go to Frankfurt to patch things up between the dealers, so that he won't lose their trust and the opportunity of earning millions to the company.

Karin is really annoyed that he has to go away again, but he promises her that he will be back the next morning, and she has more than enough to do with last-minute shopping and preparations in the house for Christmas Eve on Friday.

Already later the same evening, she talks to Gunnar again.

He complains about the meeting not developing as he had hoped, so he

doesn't expect to be home until
Thursday afternoon.

Karin therefore decides to take Anni
and Jesper, who are on their Christmas
break, to the wood Thursday morning to
buy the Christmas tree.

The children are so big now that they
should be able to manage the three of
them together, and she dares not wait
any longer.

Snow is falling and it's a tough
drive, but they manage to get there at
last and walk over to the farmer who
knows them from previous years.

He looks at them with surprise and
says, "Well, I thought you didn't come
this year."

Karin looks around, worried.

"Don't you have any more trees left?"

"No, it's always a bit of a problem
the day before Christmas Eve.
And fortunately so."

"But we usually have a tree that's somewhat bigger than those over there."

"Well, then you shouldn't have waited this long.

"Don't you usually come about a week before Christmas?"

Karin nods, and Anni and Jesper look disappointed at the trees, then Jesper bursts out, "Yes, but dad is away on business."

The farmer smiles archly at Jesper.

"Well, we can't have that ruin your Christmas, can we?"

He grabs a saw and points towards the wood.

"Come with me and we'll see if we can find exactly the right tree for you."

Jesper cheers and the three of them follow the farmer who suddenly stops by a tree.

"What about this one?"

They take a close look at the tree
while Jesper walks a little further
and touches a tall, beautiful tree.
"Or this one?"
The farmer walks up to him.
"Yes, but you have to be able to carry
it."
Karin looks carefully at the tree.
"Yes, it's much too big for the three
of us to manoeuvre into the living
room and mount on the Christmas tree
base."
The farmer looks at Jesper's
disappointed face then winks his eye
at Karin.
"Yes, but on the other hand, the
branches at the bottom are much too
thick and crooked, maybe it would be a
good idea to saw some of them off."
A little later, the farmer helps them
carry the perfectly sized tree to the
car, and the happy buyers smile while

they wish the farmer a merry Christmas
and promise to come earlier next year.
They get into the car and head home,
but even though it is only about ten
kilometres, it takes them several
hours to get through the impassable
snowfall, and they are not home until
three in the afternoon.
They immediately start to manoeuvre
the Christmas tree in place in the
living room, and Karin hurries to make
each of them a cup of hot chocolate
while they find the Christmas
decorations.
Before they know it, it's five in the
afternoon.
The phone rings, Karin answers it and
bursts out disappointedly, "No, that's
really annoying.
The children and I have fetched the
Christmas tree and …
Yes, of course, I understand.

Okay, then we just hope to see you tomorrow morning.

Yes, take care."

The children look at her with disappointment and Anni asks, "What can be so important the night before Christmas Eve?"

Karin finds it difficult to hide her annoyance but tries while she explains that some very difficult negotiations are taking place which their dad expects will not finish until later that evening, but he will take the first flight back the next day.

Jesper grumbles and says, "Is that really so important?

More important than the night before Christmas Eve?"

Karin cooks dinner while the children decorate some more, and they eat in silence.

They are all tired from the tough trip to the wood, so they go to bed rather

early on this night before Christmas
Eve.

The next morning, Karin wakes up early
and gets out of bed to get as much
done as possible before the guests
arrive in the afternoon.
She looks at her watch and glances out
the window.
It is almost one in the afternoon when
Gunnar calls and says that it has been
impossible to get a ticket home until
later, and Karin is about to cry when
she hangs up.
The guests arrive and everybody is
talking about when poor Gunnar will be
home, and Karin puts off Christmas
dinner for half an hour and then for
another half hour until her dad says
that they might as well start eating.
"It's no use to Gunnar if we have all
starved to death by the time he gets
home", he laughs.

They sit down at the table and start
to eat, but the atmosphere is not as
it usually is during Christmas dinner,
and Karin keeps repeating,
"But why doesn't he call?"
They finish eating and are about to
dance around the Christmas tree,
somewhat later than usual, when they
suddenly hear the sound of a car
coming down the quiet suburban street.
They rush to the door just as Gunner
enters, and everybody cheers.
"Now it's finally Christmas."

The Big Christmas Wish

Gitte is sitting in the insurance
company's reception area, waiting.
She looks up in anticipation every
time she hears a door opening.
Svend Nikolajsen appears, comes up to
her to greet her and asks her to
follow him to his office where she
sits down on the chair he points to.
Mr Nikolajsen looks curiously at her.
"It's been quite a while since I last
saw you.
Is everything all right?"
Gitte straightens her back.
"Well, no, that's exactly what I want
to talk to you about.
You see, I'm in desperate need for a
job and then I thought that, well, you
know so many people, maybe you could
help me?"
Mr Nikolajsen looks worriedly at her
and says that with the impending
cutbacks everywhere, that is almost

the only thing he cannot help her
with.
"A lot of people are in a tight spot
at the moment, and I'm not sure either
whether I'll keep my own job.
But you and Joergen should be all
right even though you are on
unemployment benefit?"
Gitte wrings her hands.
"Yes, we weren't so hard up
financially that we couldn't manage
for a while if one of us became
unemployed, but I've been without a
job for almost twelve months now and,
unfortunately, in August Joergen was
also laid off.
Well, he's received his usual pay for
about six months but that's coming to
an end now and Christmas is drawing
nearer, we have to pay the mortgage,
and you know …"
"Oh no, I'm sorry to hear that Joergen
has also lost his job.

Then you are certainly in for a tough time."

He suddenly sends her an encouraging smile.

"Well, I'm sure he'll soon find something else, he knows so many people."

A little later, Svend Nikolajsen sees Gitte off and wishes her a merry Christmas.

Gitte is walking down the street looking at all the amazing things beckoning at her from the shop windows while she is thinking how on earth they are going to make it through Christmas.

They cannot afford the Christmas presents, Christmas food, Christmas tree or any of the other stuff they are usually able to offer the children who love Christmas.

She walks home, downcast.

Joergen is clearing out in the garage
but when he sees Gitte, he stops and
follows her into the house.
He asks excitedly, "Well, how did it
go?"
Gitte shrugs her shoulders.
"It didn't, he doesn't even know
whether he will keep his own job.
It's a terrible world we live in.
What *are* we going to do?"
Joergen tells her that he has sent
four more job applications this
morning and that one of them was for a
job in Greenland.
Gitte looks at him, terrified.
"You can't be serious, Joergen?
Greenland?
It's not right that families have to
be torn apart just because there are
no jobs to have in this country."
"Well, I've decided that if I get the
job, I'll take it.
Then we'll see how it goes.

As it is, we cannot survive much
longer.
There's no money for the mortgage so I
guess there's a risk that the house
will foreclosed by the beginning of
the new year.
And where should we move, then?
We can't even afford hiring a moving
van."
Joergen looks close to tears and Gitte
gives him a hug.
"I don't know but we have to stick
together and even though it's
difficult, we mustn't lose heart."
Their youngest son, Frederik, comes
rushing through the door and tells
them that Mrs Nielsen, their next door
neighbour, is lying on the pavement.
They all hurry outside and Gitte
touches Mrs Nielsen's shoulder and
asks her what has happened.
Mrs Nielsen stutters something about
falling because the pavement was

slippery and asks Gitte to help her
up.

Joergen looks closely at Mrs Nielsen
and says that he doesn't think that's
a good idea and points to her hip.

"I think we need help for this.
Stay her while I get my phone."

A little later, Joergen comes out with
a pillow which he places under Mrs
Nielsen's head and a blanket which he
covers her with.

Frederik is watching intently, and at
the sound of the ambulance sirens a
crowd gathers on the pavement to see
what has happened.

"I found her", Frederik says proudly
while Gitte sends him a reproaching
look and shushes him.

But Mrs Nielsen sends him a distorted
smile and says, "Yes, I was very lucky
that you were passing by, Frederik."

Shortly after, Mrs Nielsen has been placed on a stretcher and is taken to hospital in the ambulance.
Gitte puts her arm around Frederik's shoulder and they go into the house.
Later that afternoon when the two older boys come home from school, Frederik tells them about his bravery, and they cannot help laughing at his fantastic presentation of the incident.

Mrs Nielsen, who lives alone and has no family, has given Gitte a set of keys, and Gitte has promised to bring her a toilet bag and some knitting the following day.
After that, she visits Mrs Nielsen approximately every other day.
Gitte asks Mrs Nielsen if there is anything she can bring her, and when she can come home.

A week before Christmas, Mrs Nielsen tells Gitte that she can come home the next day.

She would therefore like Gitte to receive some groceries which she has ordered for delivery in the afternoon, and of course Gitte accepts.

In the afternoon, the doorbell rings and outside is a delivery boy with some boxes with food.

He looks inquiringly at Gitte and tells her that he has been asked to deliver the groceries here.

Gitte takes the boxes with a smile and says, "Thank you, that's correct" and is about to close the door again.

The delivery boy looks at her in a strange way and says,

"That'll be seven hundred and eighty four and a half."

Gitte looks at him, terrified.

"But hasn't it been paid for?"

"No."

"But can't you just get the money next
time?"

"No, I'm sorry, I have expressly been
told that if people don't pay on
delivery, I should take the groceries
back to the shop."

Gitte feels dizzy.

This is really embarrassing.

But she doesn't have the money.

What on earth is she going to do?

She turns to the delivery boy and
says, "Just a moment", then she
fetches her mobile and calls Mrs
Nielsen.

She finally gets through to Mrs
Nielsen and explains to her that,
unfortunately, she doesn't have that
kind of money on her this close to
Christmas.

Gitte closes her mobile and asks the
young man to follow her next door.

She lets herself into Mrs Nielsen's
house, opens a drawer in the bureau,

takes out a purse and pays the
impatient delivery boy who says a
quick goodbye and runs off.

Gitte returns to the bureau to put the
purse back and sees much to her
surprise the corner of a thousand
kroner note sticking out of a folder
at the bottom.

She opens the folder and her cheeks
start blushing as she counts the many
thousand kroner notes.

Twenty seven thousand kroner.

All this money could do wonders if it
were hers.

It was exactly the amount they needed
for the mortgage, and she could buy
the boys the new winter coats they had
been talking about for so long.

She sits for a long time, dreaming.

She imagines the beautifully decorated
Christmas tree in their living room
and all the nice presents underneath
it.

She wakes up with a start at an unexpected creaking sound from the front door which is half open.

She gets up, shakes her head and immediately puts the money back in the folder.

How could she even think about it?

Gitte puts the groceries away in Mrs Nielsen's kitchen and quickly returns to her own house.

In the afternoon the next day, Gitte sees a taxi stop outside Mrs Nielsen's house and goes over there.

Mrs Nielsen seems pleased to see her and asks her whether she would like to join her for a cup of coffee.

While they are having coffee, Mrs Nielsen suddenly says that many people apparently have a hard time these days, especially with Christmas coming up.

Then she asks Gitte whether she and Joergen still haven't found new jobs.

Gitte, who has been too embarrassed to talk about it so far, now tells Mrs Nielsen that they are both looking incessantly and that, at this point, Joergen is so desperate that he has applied for a job in Greenland, which means that he will be away for six months at a time.

"What about Christmas?", Mrs Nielsen asks quietly.

Gitte looks intently at her.

"What do you mean?"

"Well, can you afford Christmas?"

Gitte briefly explains to her that, obviously, the boys won't get the new winter coats for Christmas they expect, there will also be no Christmas tree, and so on.

Mrs Nielsen looks sadly at Gitte and speaks with so much empathic warmth in her voice that Gitte almost forgets to breathe.

"You know what, I'll lend you the money for the children's winter coats, and it's no problem if you want to borrow some more.
After all, it's Christmas."
Gitte almost starts to cry when she says thank you to Mrs Nielsen.
"Thank you, that's very nice of you, and if I knew that we would have the money again if not by the beginning of the month then soon after, I believe that I would say yes, but we don't know …"
Gitte suddenly puts her hand to her forehead.
"We're so far out you wouldn't believe it, and we haven't even paid the mortgage this time.
I really don't know what to do, but we'll probably be kicked out of the house in a few months and then …"
Mrs Nielsen nods.
"Yes, I understand, of course.

I just feel so sorry for you.
But now you know that the offer
stands, you just have to let me know.
It's not like I'll be needing the
money next month or the next six
months for that matter."
Gitte gives Mrs Nielsen a hug and
tells her what a wonderful person she
is and that she mustn't forget to let
them know if she needs help with
anything. Then she goes home.

Joergen looks at her from his
computer.
"Well, there you are?
I wasn't sure where you had gone.
I've had an email and I have a job
interview tomorrow."
Gitte smiles and looks at the email on
the computer screen.
Then she gasps.
"But that's the job in Greenland."

Joergen makes a sweeping gesture as if to brush away his gloomy thoughts.

"Yes, but the pay is good, and if I'm going to live up there all by myself without any rent to pay and with all the fringe benefits I get, I'll soon be able to pay some money into the account, and maybe then we'll just about manage to avoid the most serious problems."

Gitte frowns.

"Yes, but it means you'll be away six months at a time."

"Well, that's of course the worst part of it, but if that's what it takes to get us back on our feet …
And afterwards, the situation in Denmark may have changed."

With a worried look, Gitte goes into the kitchen to prepare dinner.

The children are on their Christmas break and the next day she sits down at the kitchen table with them to make Christmas confections.

Fortunately, she remembers from her childhood how to make confections from oatmeal and apples and even though the boys don't quite understand why there is no marzipan on the table, they enjoy themselves tremendously.

Gitte hears Joergen's key in the door, and full of excitement she goes to meet him.

However, she doesn't have to ask him about the job as it is quite obvious that the interview didn't turn out the way he had hoped.

"Damn it, one moment you're too young and the next you're too old.

I was exactly the right age but, nevertheless, they preferred someone without family obligations who was prepared to commit himself for three years.

I would have agreed to that, but they didn't even ask."
Joergen tries to hide his disappointment and joins the children in the kitchen.
The boys show Joergen the confections they have made, and then they all start baking cookies.

The next day is the day before Christmas Eve. Gitte is ironing when Frederik comes storming in with her mobile which is ringing.
He looks reproachfully at her while he asks her what on earth it was doing in the basement next to the washing machine.
Gitte takes it and presents herself. Shortly after, she sits down looking completely paralysed, nodding and stuttering and answering in monosyllables.

She remains seated long after the conversation is over, tears running down her cheeks.

Joergen comes into the room and looks at her, startled, while he asks her whatever is wrong.

She throws herself at him and explains between sobs that Svend Nikolajsen had mentioned her one night at a party and that it was Henning Korsholm from the building society who had called and offered her a job, starting the first of January.

Joergen cheers from joy and starts dancing around with her and, shortly after, the boys join them and start to dance, too.

Frederik looks innocently at his mum. "Then, can I have the warm hooded coat we were looking at, after all?"

Joergen frowns while he explains that Gitte doesn't get any money until February, but Gitte glances at her

watch and says, "Hurry up and get
ready, we are going into town.
There's just something I have to do
first."
She hurries over to Mrs Nielsen's
house and rings the doorbell.
She gives Mrs Nielsen a hug and asks
her whether her offer about the loan
still stands while she chatters on
about the phone conversation and the
new job.

A little later, the four of them are
on their way to buy coats for the boys
and on the way home they stop at a
small stall to buy a Christmas tree.
Gitte also goes to the supermarket and
buys a lot of food, including candy
and wine.
On the day of Christmas Eve, Gitte
goes next door to give Mrs Nielsen a
box of chocolates and invite her over
for Christmas lunch the following day

so that she can see for herself the wonders her loan has worked.

At the lunch table, Frederik says triumphantly, "There, you see. What did I say?

I'll be damned if Christmas doesn't always come around, no matter what you say", and they all laugh out loud.

MERRY CHRISTMAS

About the author

Jette Steen lives in Odense.

She writes thrilling and dramatic social realist novels / short stories as well as theatre and film scripts and gives lectures on various topics, including how to pursue your passion, which was what she herself did after approx. 30 years in the IT business.

For more information, visit www.jettesteen.dk

www.ingramcontent.com/pod-product-compliance
Lightning Source LLC
Chambersburg PA
CBHW070749120626
46557CB00002B/509